Anna and the Baking Championship

American Civil War Adventure Prequel

Margo L. Dill

Editor-911 Kids

Copyright © 2020 Margo L. Dill

All rights reserved.

ISBN: 978-1-7353186-1-5

The characters and events portrayed in this book are fictitious. Any similarity to real persons, living or dead, is coincidental and not intended by the author.

No part of this book may be reproduced, or stored in a retrieval system, or transmitted in any form or by any means, electronic, mechanical, photocopying, recording, or otherwise, without express written permission of the publisher.

Cover design by: Editor-911 Kids, an imprint of Editor-911 Books
www.editor-911.com

Printed in the United States of America:

Published by:
Editor-911 Books
PO Box 313
Eureka, MO 63025-0313
https://www.editor-911.com

For Katie, my spunky Anna

CONTENTS

1 1
2 7
3 13
4 17
5 27
Discussion Questions 35
Author's Notes 37
About Margo L. Dill 41
About Editor-911 Books 42

1

My mind always stayed in my stories long after I closed my journal. It was the only way the pain of Pa and my brother Michael joining the Confederate Army ever went away.

Ma said her pain was like a thousand bees stinging in her chest. But stories weren't for her. She took care of missing Pa and Michael by baking delicious dishes for my younger brother and sister and me.

She held the title of the best baker in Vicksburg, well, at least in our church baking competition. Before war came to our city, she had won that title last year with her blackberry cobbler. More than anything, she wanted to teach me to bake desserts and cook fine meals. I didn't want anything to do with working in the kitchen though. I was too busy trying to write great stories like Charles Dickens.

This morning, I heard Ma banging around in the kitchen before the sun was up. She had risen extra early to prepare the kitchen for this year's dessert that would win the baking championship.

From the bed next to mine, a blonde head of curls bobbed up and down. I tried to pretend like I was still asleep.

"Anna," my little sister Sara whispered to me. "We better get up. Ma wants our help."

"Go back to sleep." I knew saying that was useless, but I couldn't stand the thought of spending the whole morning in the kitchen and would rather stay in bed.

Ma would win with or without our help, but she would insist on all of us in the kitchen with her. Usually, we had Nellie, our house servant to help us, but she'd been sick in bed for over a week. Everyone worried about her and the baby she's supposed to have next month. I didn't want anyone else to disappear from my life, especially Nellie who helped us like an auntie would. She had come to live with us along with her husband George and their son Noah, ever since my grandfather died, and his plantation was sold.

From my brother James's side of the room, I heard him imitating the sounds of cannonballs falling to the ground. He had been sleeping in our room ever since Pa and Michael had left, and General Grant tried to take our city last year. George had strung up a sheet as a partition between our beds. James said he must sleep in our room to protect us, but I knew he was scared. It was hard not to be.

"James, hush up," I said, realizing then and there I couldn't stay in bed any longer with these two as my siblings. Standing up and stretching, I changed out of my nightclothes and helped Sara with hers.

Running down the steps, taking them two at a time, since Ma couldn't see me and scold me for not acting like a lady, I sighed and thought about turning right at the bottom of the stairs, into our parlor. Since Pa left, Ma forced me to keep my journal in there at night, so I didn't spend hours writing in it by candlelight in my room.

"Let's go." Sara jumped down the last two steps, holding her ragdoll Betty tightly with one hand and with the other tugging me. "We have to help, or we won't beat Mrs. Franklin."

"That old busybody's been so busy bragging that her recipe is the best that she hasn't had any time to make it. She won't win."

This year, it was more important than ever to win the prize for two reasons. Reason number one concerned mean, old Mrs. Franklin and her dumb son, Stuart. No one in my family appreciated living next door to Mrs. Franklin, except that she was married to our doctor who had a kind heart. Her daughter Molly had a newborn baby, and Baby Peter was awful cute, but she lived in a house a few blocks away with her husband. Lately, Ma had been helping Dr. Franklin with a few tasks like Molly used to do, and he paid Ma a fee in return.

Only half of the Franklin family was kind—Molly and Dr. Franklin. The other two—I wished they would cross the Mississippi and never come back! Stuart and my brother were constantly engaged in fist fights. Mrs. Franklin always looked down her nose at us because she thought she was better. She didn't approve of the way we treated our servants like they were a part of our family. She had several slaves, and she was wicked mean to all of them. My ma and pa gave George and Nellie a place to live and paid them a very small salary, although they told no one about that except for Michael and me.

One time, when George accidentally dropped a basket of clean clothes on the grass, Mrs. Franklin yelled over to Ma: "That Negro of yours is so clumsy. What will his punishment be?"

I heard Mrs. Franklin whipped her slaves, just like they did out on the plantations.

She had continued. "If Olivia was as careless as him, she wouldn't see the light of day for weeks."

I could not understand wanting to hurt another person like that. No wonder Mrs. Franklin's slaves were always trying to run away.

The biggest reason I wanted Ma to win didn't have anything to do with beating Mrs. Franklin. Winning the baking contest meant there was a $2 prize! We needed the $2 more than ever with Pa and Michael both serving in the army, and the money they sent home taking longer and longer to get to us. Ma's money jar was running out of dollars; only coins filled it now. The prices in the general store kept going up and up. Yankees blocked our supplies from reaching us and sometimes stole them for their own soldiers. I couldn't wait for this war to be over and for life to return to normal in Vicksburg.

"It's about time you girls made it down here to the kitchen." Ma did not have her pretty smile. Strands of hair fell from her usually neat bun. "Hurry up and grab the cocoa powder for me, Anna. We are so far behind if we are to have a fresh chocolate cake frosted and ready for the judging at noon."

"Yes, ma'am," I said and looked on the shelf for what she needed.

"Ma," James called as soon as he entered the kitchen. He still wore his nightclothes, even though Ma liked us to change before coming downstairs. "I'm starving like a bear who hasn't had any honey for a week."

"James, you can get some porridge from the pot on the stove and go on. We are busy with the cake this morning."

"I have to serve myself?"

"Oh goodness, James." He infuriated me! "Should we make your last name Franklin now? Have you forgotten what it's like to be a member of the Green family? You are eleven years old and more than capable of helping yourself."

"Stop lecturing me, Anna. You are only two years older!"

He grabbed a bowl from the cupboard and sloshed over to the stove. The large pot of porridge bubbled; and as he lifted the lid, steam poured out. My stomach rumbled, as I hadn't had any breakfast yet either. Ma had put me right to work. "Ma, can I have a bowl?"

"Me also," Sara asked.

"Girls, we have no time for foolery or bad manners. We ask: May I please have a bowl? Anna, I would think with your obsession with the written word that you could manage to properly ask for some breakfast. But never you mind that. We must get busy." Ma cracked an egg on the side of the bowl when a loud knock sounded at the door.

The sun was barely peeking into the windows yet, and so I wondered who could possibly be coming to our house so early.

We all stopped moving and looked at each other. A sinking feeling in my stomach erupted through my body, and I could see the same happening with James and Ma. Sara was too young to understand, but what we all worried about was a knock this early meant that someone was coming to tell us terrible news about Pa or Michael.

The knock sounded again, and Ma moved toward the door.

2

We heard some loud stomping on our front porch and then a screeching voice from outside the door. "Hurry up, Rachel," Mrs. Franklin called.

I breathed a sigh of relief. What did she want? She was probably over here to distract us or to steal our batter.

Ma opened the door, and we heard her say, "Well, Mildred, what a nice surprise."

How could Ma say that to Mrs. Franklin?

She smelled like onions and waddled like a penguin I had read about in a book. Or at least what I imagined a waddling penguin to look like. Ma and Mrs. Franklin made their way back into the kitchen. Mrs. Franklin's hair was pulled back so tightly from her face that it made wrinkles from her eye sockets to her ears.

"Children, let's all say hello to Mrs. Franklin," Ma commanded. Since Ma worked for Dr. Franklin, I supposed she had to be nice. Just yesterday, Ma had made some medicine and creams for him.

The three of us looked at each other and muttered hello. We would surely get a scolding from Ma once Mrs. Franklin left.

"Never you mind." The old busybody waved her hands in front of her face. "I have no time to talk, and I do apologize for interrupting what is sure to be quite an entry into the baking championship." She rolled her eyes while speaking, and I knew she didn't mean that nicely.

I wanted to take one of the eggs near the bowl and throw it at her head. James looked like he was about to.

Mrs. Franklin wagged her finger. "Dr. Franklin sent a message that you need to come quick, Rachel, with the salve you made for burns yesterday. Mr. Adams called on my husband a while ago because their slave boy burnt his arm while stoking fires this morning, and Dr. Franklin thought he had some of that burn salve in his bag. But I suppose he has misplaced it. He needs you to take it and deliver it."

This didn't sound like a true story to me. It sounded like Mrs. Franklin was trying to give Ma some task to attend to and keep her from baking our cake. Was our busybody neighbor worried that she would be defeated once again? Why couldn't

Stuart deliver the salve? Or James. Maybe Noah could do it since Ma had given George the day off to take care of Nellie. Everyone knew where the Adamses lived by the courthouse.

"Why, Mildred, if I didn't know better, I would say you're sending me on an errand that your son or mine or Olivia could easily do." Ma wiped her hands on her apron; then she opened a cupboard and moved some bottles around. She popped her head around the cupboard door and waved a bottle in the air. "I have it right here. I'll send James or Noah."

James took a huge bite of porridge and said, "I'm not going."

Ma put her hands on her hips. "Mind your manners, young man."

I stepped in to convince James to cooperate. Ma could not go on this errand. We needed her here to bake this cake! "Maybe you can help with the burn, James," I said. "Learn some doctoring, and—"

Mrs. Franklin stomped her foot. "Wait a moment! Y'all will listen. My husband specifically sent word that Mrs. Green was to come herself and bring the salve. The burn must be simply awful, and he needs another adult, who understands a bit of medicine, as impossible as that seems for a woman, to help him. We do not go against my husband's wishes."

I laughed; her head whipped around, and she glared at me. "What is so funny, young lady?" she asked, peering down her beaky nose.

"You are constantly going against your husband's wishes, ma'am." I didn't want the manners lecture from Ma, so I had added ma'am.

"Anna, where are your manners?" Ma scolded.

James smirked at me, and I wanted to drop that bowl of porridge on his head.

"Ma'am," I cleared my throat and tried to start out slow. Then forged ahead because I wanted to get this out. It was crucial to our family! "You're constantly going against your husband's wishes. When the Yankees tried to take over our city last year, he told you to stay put, stay at home. Our soldiers would protect us. I heard him tell Pa a few weeks later that you left him and Stuart and went to your mother's in New Orleans." I batted my eyelashes at her. "Of course, none of us even realized you were gone." That was a lie. I would have to ask for forgiveness later. Every single one of us definitely noticed that she was gone, and we had wanted to celebrate.

It had been so peaceful, except for the Yankees fighting over our city. But our soldiers had held them back, and Grant failed. And he would fail again and again because we were strong and united in Vicksburg. We loved our city!

"Enough of this!" Mrs. Franklin interrupted. "Mrs. Green, are you following your superior's request, or should we make other arrangements for a nurse?"

Ma untied her apron as Mrs. Franklin spoke. It was already strange for Ma to work as an assistant to Dr. Franklin, but now she was practically jumping when Mrs. Franklin told her to. The war was doing strange things to people. Next thing we knew, Ma would be working at one of the army hospitals, and we would have to take care of ourselves. I couldn't imagine anything worse. How would we ever survive without her? I didn't know how to cook. I barely knew how to sew. And my brother never listened to anything I said.

Ma turned to me and held my shoulders. "Listen, Anna, you will have to finish mixing this cake and bake it. We have no time to spare if we will make it to the baking contest on time. The cake must cool before we put on the frosting, or it will be ruined. You know how to make a cake, right? This is very important. I need to count on you."

"Yes, Ma." I wondered if I could remember the recipe but sounded like I was as confident as James when he leaped across the creek in one jump last summer. "I know how to bake a cake. I will not let us down. We will win first place and the money," I whispered the last part so that the old busybody would not hear.

Ma kissed my cheek, leaned down, and hugged Sara who had been unusually quiet during this entire ordeal. Sara was frightened of Mrs. Franklin.

She had seen her beat her slave Olivia one time, and Sara had hardly spoken a word since then whenever Mrs. Franklin was around. Ma waved at James who scowled at Mrs. Franklin from his seat at the table with his head almost buried in his bowl of porridge. Ma tied her bonnet and went out with a gust of spring breeze making its way to the kitchen when she opened the front door.

As the door shut, my brain whirled into action, wishing I'd have paid more attention when I helped bake a cake for my brother's birthday before he joined the army. How hard would it be to remember Ma's famous recipe?

3

Two hours later, Ma returned from aiding Dr. Franklin, and we managed to have a chocolate cake cooling on the table. If I had made the cake correctly, we would probably win the contest. Baking chocolate into a cake didn't happen often. Most people made white cake and added the chocolate in the icing or as a drink. But we wanted to be special, and I loved Ma's chocolate cake recipe.

Sara had helped me measure and mix the ingredients. Plus, she and I had decided when we thought the cake had finished baking. There was a teeny tiny worry in my mind. When we had licked the batter, it tasted differently than it usually did. But, sometimes, Ma didn't let us lick the batter when she baked, and so maybe my memory was just wrong. Maybe ours tasted exactly like cake batter before it was baked into a delicious dessert.

James had laughed at us and said, "You will lose. You're allowing a six year old to decide when the cake is done?"

But I shooed him out of the kitchen and told him to collect some firewood. I wished so badly that Nellie could come from her quarters to help us. But she was hardly ever awake long enough to even eat, so I didn't want to bother her with questions.

I was also concerned about a rule Reverend Lohrs's wife had made last year. The baking championship rules now specifically said that the female of the household had to bake the dessert entry herself. This rule was made because some families let their servants do the baking, and Mrs. Lohrs didn't think this was fair.

Sara and I wondered if this rule would mean our family could be disqualified this year because I was not the female of the household. If my sneaky suspicion was correct, and Ma had to be present in our kitchen when the cake was baked, then we knew Mrs. Franklin would tell everyone that Ma had been out helping Dr. Franklin. Maybe this was the very reason why she had sent Ma to deliver the salve. We would have to cross our fingers and hope that Ma being here during some of the baking would still count.

Ma hung up her bonnet and grabbed her apron. "I am happy to see a cake in the middle of the table," she said as she tied the apron around her. "Is it cool?"

I shrugged my shoulders, and Sara asked, "How do we tell?"

Taking my sister's hand, Ma led her to the table and told her to stick out her pointer finger. My sister did. "Gently touch the cake with your finger. Does it feel warm?"

"A little."

"Then we'll make the frosting and wait a bit longer to put it on the cake. I'm proud of you children. I was not sure what I would come home to, and I suppose that Dr. Franklin did need my help with the poor boy at the Adamses' home. The only serious injury is the boy's arm." She took a mixing bowl off the shelf. "Everyone was frantic, and Mrs. Adams has discovered she is newly with child. She is very nauseous and vomiting quite often." Ma went on, but I stopped listening.

Sara hummed to herself, also seeming to ignore Ma's ramblings. I knew that Ma missed talking to Pa ever since he had become a soldier. We heard rumors that our army was losing the war, especially since Grant was allowing slaves to fight in the North. How could we let our beautiful state or any of the South be taken by the Yanks? Pa was just trying to help defend our home.

We watched Ma add some confectioners' sugar, butter, and cocoa to the bowl as well as coffee and vanilla. She mixed and mixed until the consistency was that of frosting. I wanted to stick my finger in it and taste. My mouth watered, but Ma would slap my hand, and then I would not get any sweets at the baking championship. I could wait. Even James knew not to stick his finger in the bowl of frosting when he came into the kitchen. I saw him eyeing the bowl, and Ma glared at him.

The smell of the cake baking had made me mighty hungry. I wished we would have made a smaller one for ourselves.

I couldn't wait to be done with this baking. I wanted to finish my story I had started a few days ago about a soldier in the war. The soldier's words to his commander rang through my head, almost like he was talking to me. I could not share this with anyone in my family, or they would think I was looney. One time, I had told Pa that my characters talked to me when I wrote about them and even when I didn't. He said that made me special. My heart longed so much to see him again.

"Time to frost the cake, children, and then we will wash up and make our way to church with our dessert. I am thrilled how you helped this morning, Anna. It seems like all my hard lessons are finally making their way into your mind."

I beamed from Ma's praise because it did not come easily or often, especially since Pa and Michael had left. Yet, I kept my fingers crossed behind my back that the cake tasted as delicious as it looked, and the funny taste was not in the batter, only in our minds. I hoped the praise Ma gave me now did not turn into disappointment later this afternoon.

4

Parents and children milled around in front of the church because the weather was bright, sunny, and warm for the middle of March. It appeared no one had anything better to do on a Saturday than bake a dessert and enter the contest. A warm breeze blew the ribbons on my braids as I shyly waved at Albert who stood almost as tall as Reverend Lohrs. I was so glad Albert was not old enough to fight in the war. He was Mrs. Franklin's nephew, but I tried to ignore that fact.

I saw Amanda Buckley calling to Albert, and my stomach sank until he grinned and rolled his eyes at me. This made me giggle, but then James made kissing noises on his hand. "You love Albert!"

"Stop it, James. He is my friend." Little brothers were so annoying.

Ma greeted our neighbors while my siblings and I followed behind her, smiling and only speaking to the adults if we were spoken to. Many of the boys and girls we went to school with also accompanied their parents; and most people seemed eager to get the baking contest judged, so the eating portion could begin.

When we entered the church, tables had been placed in the back of the last wooden pew; and one was already filled with cookies, cakes, and pies.

"I would like to be left alone with all of these delicious treats. I'd gobble them the way a wolf gobbles his rabbit dinner," James whispered to me.

"You are disgusting," I said. "You need to keep your hands off, James, or we will be disqualified, and you will be in the corner of the kitchen all night with no treats in sight."

Near the table, Mrs. Franklin and Stuart argued over what looked like a pink-frosted cake with white frilly designs down the side of it. I heard Stuart say, "Olivia said I could try some when she was finished."

"Hush up, Stuart. I made this cake with my own two hands, and you are not having any of it, young man." Mrs. Franklin's hands were now on her hips, and I bet they were never in any cake batter this morning.

Did I hear Stuart say that Olivia had made their cake?

When Mrs. Franklin saw us nearing with our entry, she sneered.

I wondered by the looks of the pink frilly cake if Olivia really had baked it. I could see how absolutely perfect and beautiful it was. Mrs. Franklin didn't lift a finger at her house, so how would she have been able to make such a pretty cake on her own? I had no proof that she didn't. And I knew Stuart would never tell the truth, even if he wanted to, because he would be punished for tattling on Mrs. Franklin. I prayed a quick prayer that our cake at least tasted better than Olivia's—I meant the Franklins'.

As we set our cake down, Reverend Lohrs's wife explained how the contest would be judged. I remembered from last year, as I was sure Ma did, but we listened politely anyway. Mrs. Lohrs was a plump, kind, young woman, about the same age as Ma, and she moved her hands nervously while she talked. Her daughter Emily, who was the same age as Sara, grabbed my sister's hands, and they started skipping and singing in the back of the church. Then they stopped and played toss with Betty the doll.

"The contest rules say that each entry can receive up to ten points," Mrs. Lohrs said over Sara and Emily's singing.

"Hush up, girls," Mrs. Franklin barked, and they both stopped, looking like they wanted to cry.

Mrs. Lohrs continued, "The majority of those points will be awarded based on the taste. The decorations will only be a deciding factor if both entries taste absolutely perfect."

Last year, Ma's blackberry cobbler had received a perfect ten while the Franklins' apple cake received a nine. Mrs. Franklin said we won because of our obnoxious decorations; however, there were no decorations on our dessert or hers, so that made no sense.

I kept my fingers crossed behind my back. Mrs. Franklin could not beat us this year even though the cake, made by Olivia or not, looked like a dream. If we won the prize money, maybe Ma would not have to work so hard with Dr. Franklin.

"Rachel," Mrs. Franklin called over the chatter from the other congregants sitting in the pews with their family members. "We were not sure you would make it here today, as you are almost late."

"Wouldn't you have liked that, you old busybody?" James said under his breath.

"I heard that." Stuart pointed his finger at James. "Ma, he called you an old busybody."

"She is!" James yelled and ran toward Stuart.

"She is not!" Stuart shouted back.

All eyes watched the two boys to see what would happen next. Ma said, "Anna, please stop your brother before the boys knock into one of the tables and destroy everyone's hard work today."

By the time I reached the boys, Stuart had James in a head lock and was rubbing his hair, saying, "Take it back. My ma is not an old busybody."

James could not speak, as he was being choked by Stuart. It looked like perhaps my brother's face was turning a little purple.

The Reverend, tall and lean, stood nearest to the sparring boys and clapped his hands so loudly, the

Made in the USA
Monee, IL
08 July 2021

noise rang throughout the rafters. Stuart stopped just long enough that James got free and ran behind me. "Stop it, James!" I scolded. "Let us go sit down and say a quick prayer that the cake is as delicious as it looks."

"Fine," James said and crossed his arms.

As I led him to a pew, my eyes stayed on Ma who rearranged the entries, as Mrs. Lohrs directed her. Sara stood as close to Ma as she could because Mrs. Franklin had scolded her and Emily again. The old busybody now held Betty in her arms, shaking her as she talked at the children. James stuck his tongue out at Stuart.

"Can't you stop for one day? This is important," I said to my brother.

James pointed at Mrs. Franklin. "She's not stopping, so why should I?"

We sat down, and Ma and Sara, finally with Betty back, came soon after. Music played from the piano while some families sang the same hymns that we sang on Sunday morning. My stomach rumbled and twisted with hunger from the smell of the delicious desserts and from fear of how the cake would taste. I didn't want to let Ma down.

Reverend Lohrs introduced the judges, one was our schoolteacher and the other Mrs. Lohrs. Then he asked for everyone to leave the sanctuary while the judging took place. Everyone stood up, although some people walked slowly, like they didn't want to leave, including my brother.

"Move along, James," the Reverend said. "No judging will begin until everyone is outside."

While we waited for what seemed like hours for the judges to finish their tasting, a game of Knurr and Spell broke out, and Sara, Ma, and I sat on the sidelines. I watched Albert hit the knurr the farthest and James argue that Albert was a cheater. I wanted Ma to make James behave, but she kept wringing her hands and seemed distracted.

"Anna?"

"Yes, Ma."

"I wonder about that errand I was sent on while baking this morning."

"I thought you said they needed you."

"Yes, yes."

My stomach twisted even more than it had after Ma's statement. Now she was doubting what had happened this morning, just as I had since Mrs. Franklin first came to our door. Soon, we would all know the baking championship results, and I could stop worrying. "Cross your fingers," I said to Sara. And she did without even asking me why.

About an hour later, the Reverend finally appeared at the door and waved everyone in. We all hurried to sit in the pews. "I wish we were this quick to come in on a Sunday morning," the Reverend joked.

Many people chuckled, but I could not find it in my heart to laugh. My nerves felt like they had bolts of lightning attached to them.

"We will start with third place," Mrs. Lohrs said. "Third place goes to the Buckley family."

Amanda jumped up to accompany her ma and grandma, and I watched Albert's face carefully to see if he was as fond of her as she was of him. I hoped not, even though I could never reveal how I felt about Albert.

Our schoolteacher was next at the podium. With her loud and booming voice that she always used to correct students, especially James and Stuart, she announced, "Second place goes to--," I prayed she would say Mrs. Franklin's name and not ours. "The Herberts."

My stomach flipped. It was surprising that Olivia's beautiful cake, if we were to believe Stuart, did not win second place. I knew firsthand what a great baker she was, and she made very few mistakes. Besides, Mrs. Franklin wouldn't allow her to! I bit my fingernails, starting to worry that maybe our cake would not be a winner at all. Maybe I had made a mistake. Ma twisted a piece of her hair and looked at me with wide eyes.

Maybe the Reverend and his wife had realized Mrs. Franklin was a cheat, and that was why they did not choose her for second place this year.

The Reverend walked to the podium with a smile on his face, although it seemed strained. I held my breath as he said, "And first place goes to the Franklins."

James jumped up. "They're a bunch of cheats. Olivia made that cake."

No one seemed to pay any attention to James as Mrs. Franklin walked up to the altar to receive her prize, although there was a lot of murmuring in the sanctuary. James started to follow Mrs. Franklin up to the altar, but Ma dragged him by the collar and out the door. Tears sprang into my eyes and Sara's also.

We did not win anything. What was wrong with our cake? No one else had tried to bake a chocolate cake, and I had used Ma's recipe. Right? I went through all the ingredients that I had put in. I was sure I had measured correctly and carefully. Maybe the judges didn't like chocolate. I was determined I would ask one of them what was wrong with the cake. I would do better. I might have let Ma down this time, but I wouldn't next time.

As everyone headed to the back of the sanctuary where the desserts sat, I headed up with Sara to see the Reverend. "Oh, Anna," he said. "I heard that your ma was called away this morning, and you had to finish baking the cake." He pointed to Sara and me.

Nodding, I blinked back any more tears from coming out. "Sir, were we disqualified for breaking a rule?"

"No, no." He sighed and then whispered, "There was something wrong with your cake. It tasted well, salty, not sweet, and the consistency was not correct. Do you think you could have substituted salt for sugar in the middle of the chaos this morning?"

I carefully thought back to baking this morning. For once, my head had not been lost in my stories. "I don't know, sir," I said. "We do not keep the salt in the same place as the sugar, and I remember taking the sugar tin from the shelf and measuring."

"Hmmm," the Reverend said. "I can't be sure. Baking is not my specialty. Just tasting the delicious desserts." He patted me on the back and rubbed his chin as I waited anxiously for him to tell me something more. "Mrs. Lohrs was the one who thought maybe salt had been used instead of sugar. She's the most excellent baker I know, of course, so it might be worth investigating, Anna."

A sinking feeling began in my throat and went to the tips of my toes. What was Reverend Lohrs trying to tell me? I had a suspicion again that the Franklins had cheated because it was the only way they could beat us. I rushed out to where Ma still had a hold of James. Sara held my hand, and I practically dragged her along, hurrying.

"Ma, I'm so sorry," I said. "But I think there's an explanation. We must hurry home. I need to check our tins. Maybe I used the wrong ingredients."

"We were so careful, Anna," my sister said in a quiet voice.

"We were," I said.

As Ma followed, hardly saying a word, I noticed that Dr. Franklin and Mrs. Franklin were a few feet ahead of us on the road with no Stuart in sight.

5

Ma held Sara's hand while we walked down the road toward our house and kept her eyes on James, who shuffled his feet only a few steps ahead. Sara's doll dragged behind her. Everyone looked so tired. I thought the baking championship was supposed to be fun!

Ma broke the quiet. "Tell me again what the Reverend said, Anna."

"He said our cake tasted salty, not sweet. He also knew about you being called away by Dr. Franklin. I think he was trying to give me a message."

"A message about what?" Sara asked, almost skipping to keep up with Ma.

I shrugged my shoulders and said the next bit carefully, as I didn't want Ma to accuse me of being a sore loser. "A message that even though the

Franklins had the winning cake and claimed Mrs. Franklin made it, there was foul play."

"You are looney," James shouted back to me. "The only foul play is that you don't know how to bake a cake at thirteen years old!"

"That's enough, James Green, you will be in the corner when we return home." Ma let go of Sara's hand and grabbed mine. "You should forget about this. It was too much pressure on you this morning. I was beside myself about winning again, but really, that is not what is important. Your pa's money will make it home to us soon. I have some in our jar still. Dr. Franklin paid me this morning for my time. There will be plenty."

I nodded, but as soon as I returned home, I was getting to the bottom of this mystery. I didn't think I made a mistake. I would prove it to Ma!

When we were close enough to see our porch, I took off running, faster than even James.

"Where's the fire?" he asked, using an expression our pa used when one of us looked to be in a big hurry.

I ran up our front porch steps and burst into the front door, hurrying back to the kitchen when I caught sight of a person trying to rush out our back door. I sprinted and grabbed the shirt tail of…

"Stuart!" I yelled. "Why are you in our house? What do you have in your hand under that cloth?"

I grabbed it from his hand, but he held on tight. We struggled until he fell backwards and down the couple steps out our back door. I closed the door and locked it—I hoped he would be fine. It wasn't that big of a drop from our back door to the grass.

As the rest of my family came in, I took the cloth off the object that Stuart had been trying to sneak out. It was our sugar tin! I looked up at the shelf where our spices and dry goods were kept, but there was another sugar container there that looked exactly like ours. We didn't have two sugar containers. This was a metal set that Ma had purchased at the general store. Many of our neighbors had the same metal set, including the Franklins.

Then an idea popped in my mind, and I realized what was happening! I wanted to tell Ma immediately, but she had gone outside to see if Stuart was hurt from falling down the stairs.

I plopped down at the table with the container that Stuart had under the cloth and removed the lid.

I stuck my finger in and tasted a mixture of salty and sweet. There was not only sugar in the mix, but also salt! Examining it closer, there was probably more salt than sugar. "James," I said. "Guard this with your life."

He gave me a salute.

Reaching up, I grabbed the other tin labeled sugar off the shelf and opened it. I sifted my fingers through and smelled it. Then I stuck a finger in and tasted it. Pure sugar, nothing strange in this one. When had the Franklins switched the containers and put the one with salt and sugar on our shelf, so we would use it in our cake this morning? Why hadn't I noticed that when I was baking earlier?

All day, I knew that the Franklins had been cheating, but I thought they had called Ma away to give them an advantage. They were even more deceitful than that! They didn't want Ma, an experienced baker, to notice the sugar and salt mixture. She definitely would have if she wouldn't have been called away to "help" Dr. Franklin.

"Ma, come quick and bring Stuart," I yelled out the back door

With Ma pushing him with her hand, Stuart walked in. His arms were crossed, and he looked like he wanted to be anywhere but in our kitchen.

"I know what happened! Stuart switched our sugar tin with a tin of salt and sugar mixture yesterday. Just now, he came back to switch it to the original one with our sugar. This way, everyone would blame Sara and me for baking a bad tasting cake. Of course, it tasted strange. There was too much salt and not enough sugar!" I pointed my finger at Stuart. "Luckily, I caught him, just now, trying to switch the tins back. Now, no one can blame Sara and me." I crossed my arms and glared at him, wondering what lie he would try to tell.

"She is looney," Stuart said. I was tired of people always calling me looney. They were the looney ones. "I was in the kitchen because, ummm, because—"

"Because you are a big cheater." Now James pointed his finger at Stuart's chest.

"That's enough, everyone," Ma said. "Stuart, why are you in our house?"

His face turned bright red, and he said, "I am not telling you, Mrs. Green."

"I see." Ma looked at the container that Stuart had been trying to take out of our house when I caught him. She stuck her finger in there and tasted the powder. "Yes, Anna appears to be correct. There is salt and sugar mixed in here." She sighed and placed her hand on my shoulder. "And of course, you didn't realize this earlier because you are new to baking cakes, Anna. I suppose you and Sara did not lick the bowl when you finished pouring the batter in the pan?"

"Umm, yes, well, we did, but I thought maybe the strange taste was because we hadn't tried chocolate batter before."

Ma grinned at me. "I see we have many more lessons to learn before you are ready for your own household." I grinned but wished she would not have reminded me of how much work I still had to do. All this time away from my writing was terribly difficult. My soldier character waited for me to write him out of a battle safely and send him home to his family.

I finally realized when Stuart must have switched the containers. "Stuart, my guess is while we were out in our garden last night, and I saw you playing with your ball at the side of our house, you snuck in when we were not paying attention and swapped these containers."

James joined in. "And your mean, old ma looked for an excuse to call our ma away!"

Stuart shook his head no, but that's exactly what had happened. I knew it. It wasn't my fault. Sara and I didn't bake a bad cake. Well, we did, but only because the ingredients had been changed without our knowledge.

Ma grabbed Stuart by the hand. "Come on, Stuart, I need to have a talk with your ma. We won't tell the Reverend about this new discovery. The contest is over for this year. But your ma will most definitely not be entering the championship contest next year. I don't want everyone to find out about your cheating ways, but I will make an announcement at church if I have to."

"Yes, ma'am," Stuart said and lumbered out after Ma and the salt-sugar container.

"So now what?" James asked.

"I know exactly what we can do while Ma is gone." I had to prove that I did know how to bake, so I could have fewer lessons in the kitchen. Besides, we had all been too sad to try any of the desserts after Reverend Lohrs had announced the contest results. And eating sweets had been something to look forward to all day.

I grabbed the mixing bowl and measured carefully, tasting the ingredients before putting them in the bowl. Once they were all mixed in, the three of us put our fingers in the bowl and tasted the batter. I hoped Ma would not be angry about us baking another cake since the general store had been short of flour last week. James was the first to speak. "That tastes delicious."

He started to put his whole hand in the batter, but I stopped him. We poured the cake batter into a pan and stuck it in the oven.

Ma returned with quite a tale to share about how Mrs. Franklin said she didn't know anything about Stuart's plan. "Then on my way out, Mrs. Franklin had insisted on a cup of tea and a piece of Olivia's winning cake. It was a dream." She licked her lips, and Sara burst out laughing. I hoped Ma would say the same about our cake now baking in the oven.

"Finally, I told Mildred I couldn't sit around eating sweets all day, and as I grabbed my bonnet, Stuart shouted that his ma had paid him twenty-five cents for switching the tins yesterday evening."

What a fortune! I thought.

The smell of my cake baking made my stomach grumble.

"It looks like I'll still be working for Dr. Franklin some more," Ma said.

"I am happy to help with Sara and James," I said. "I know we all have to join together while we fight the Yankees."

"The war is sad," Ma said.

"I hope it ends soon," Sara said.

As I removed a perfectly shaped and wonderfully smelling chocolate cake from the oven, I wondered how else the war could possibly affect us. Grant had already failed to take Vicksburg, and General Lee said our army was getting stronger every day, even though some gossip said the opposite. I'd pray that we would all be back together this summer, and how surprised Pa and Michael would be to see my baking skills improved!

DISCUSSION QUESTIONS

1. Why does Anna hope her family will win the baking championship this year? Give two reasons.

2. Do you think that Dr. Franklin really needed Anna's ma's help at the Adamses' house? Or was that part of the plan to help the Franklins cheat?

3. How would you feel if you were Anna and had to bake the cake by yourself for the first time?

4. What is special about a chocolate cake in 1863?

5. In the southern United States in 1863, slavery was legal. How do you feel about the mention of slaves in this story? Why did the author include slavery in the story?

6. Compare and contrast the way that Anna and Mrs. Franklin treated people.

7. Who do you think actually baked the Franklins' cake? Give two reasons for your answer.

8. How did Anna feel when it was announced that their cake won nothing in the championship? Find a sentence in the story that supports your answer.

9. Do you agree with Ma to not tell Reverend Lohrs about the cheating this year? Why or why not?

10. What would you do if you found out someone cheated in a contest?

AUTHOR'S NOTES

Want to read more about Anna, her family, and mean, old Mrs. Franklin?

To find out what happens in the summer of 1863 to Anna and her family during a 47-day siege, where Anna is forced to live in a cave with Mrs. Franklin and Yankees bomb the city day and night, then you can continue reading the American Civil War Adventure series book one, *Finding My Place: One Girl's Strength at Vicksburg*, available in print, where books are sold; on the publisher's website, White Mane Kids; or on www.margoldill.com, where you can get an autographed copy.

Finding My Place: One Girl's Strength at Vicksburg is available as an e-book. You can read the e-book for free if you are a Kindle Unlimited member! It is a full-length middle-grade novel.

Do you know anyone who would like this story?

If you enjoyed this story, please consider telling a friend, parent, child, teacher, librarian, or grandparent. Word of mouth is one of the best ways to help an author get the word out about her books.

You can also leave a review on Amazon.com. Reviews are social proof and help sell books!

What is Knurr and Spell?

In this story, while Anna and the rest of her family wait for the judges to announce the winners of the baking championship, she watches a game of Knurr and Spell. Knurr and Spell is an old game that was played with a stick and a small ball. The ball is called a knurr and made of hard wood; or as the game progressed through the years, the knurr was covered with leather for safety reasons. The spell is made of wood and might remind you of a long-handled stick with a short paddle on the end. Some people might compare it to golf more than any other modern-day game. Players hit the knurr with the spell toward a target.

What people say about *Finding My Place:*

"This is such a captivating read! I couldn't stop thinking about Anna and what would happen to her family next." ~Michelle Cornish, 5 stars on Amazon

"This book was uniquely researched and written as an American Civil War Adventure story. Though designed as an adventure story, it is an educational story for all ages as well. The intriguing story line will not allow you to stop turning the pages, as you yearn to find out what happens next. The story tells of a young teenage girl and her family's experiences and hardships, both emotional and physical." ~Michelle Robertson, Readers' Favorite

"As a former teacher, this is one book I know I would include in my classroom library today." ~Dianna Graveman, 5 stars on Amazon.

"This book is very well-written. It shows historical events in the Civil War era through the eyes of a 13-year old girl. Middle-grade readers should enjoy this, and it will show them that history doesn't have to be boring and dry." ~Michaela, 4 stars on Amazon

"I picked up this book recently as I'm interested in the Civil War era. This short novel is well-researched and entertaining. It clearly illustrates the deprivations and horrors endured by families during the siege of Vicksburg through the eyes of a spunky and likable heroine. As another reviewer observed, it would be an excellent teaching resource for a study of the Civil War." ~Pat Wahler, historical fiction award-winning author

"What makes *Finding My Place* stand out from other books is that Anna lives in Vicksburg in the South. It's unusual to read a story about the Civil War of people who lived in the South. However, the challenges she faces will appeal to kids, regardless of where they live. The book is well researched, and I loved learning about the historical tidbits the author weaves into the story."
~Sarah W., 5 stars on Amazon

ABOUT MARGO L. DILL

Margo L. Dill has loved writing since she was a kid. When she became an elementary school teacher and then a parent, she kept writing stories for both kids and adults. She's been published in numerous magazines, newspapers, and ezines, such as *Fun with Kidz, Highlights for Children, The Chicago Tribune, Pockets Magazine*, plus *WOW! Women On Writing*, where she is currently the managing editor and an online writing instructor. She is the author of *Maggie Mae, Detective Extraordinaire: The Case of the Missing Cookies; Listen, Lucy! Listen! A Red Ribbon Week Adventure* (Fall 2020); and *It's Not Just Academics: A Guide to Teaching Kids Health, Communication, and Real Life Skills* (Fall or Winter 2020). She lives in St. Louis, MO, with her daughter and lab mix dog, Sudsi. Find out more about Margo at www.margoldill.com.

ABOUT EDITOR-911 BOOKS

Editor-911 Books publishes entertaining and informative books for children of all ages and adults, specifically writers and parents. Owned by Margo L. Dill, we are located in St. Louis, MO, and on the web at https://www.editor-911.com. The three imprints under Editor-911 Books are Editor-911 Kids, Editor-911 Romance, and Editor-911 Knowledge.

Other Editor-911 Kids Books

Read-Aloud Stories with Fred, Vol 1., by Fred Olds

Read-Aloud Stories with Fred, Vol. 1 is a collection of three bedtime stories for children. Bedtime is a special time for you and your children or grandchildren! One part of your routine may be reading aloud! These three delightful stories from author Fred Olds, all in Volume 1, present the adventures a child longs for while providing parents and grandparents a wise voice similar to Aesop's fables from when they were kids.

"Ben and the Terrible Red Card" tells the story of Ben, who talks to readers about why his teacher doesn't understand him, and he keeps getting in trouble at school. "The Hobbling Hermit" reminds us that when you have a friend—especially one who is a smart, tiny mouse—all your problems can be solved. Finally, this volume of *Read-Aloud Stories with Fred* introduces children to Sammy, who lives in the jungle with his mother and can talk to animals in "Sammy and the Cross-eyed Crow." During this adventure, Sammy decides to help a friend in need which requires him to break a promise to his mom and face some consequences.

These stories are for fun before you say good night to your little ones, but you'll also find plenty of conversations around these tales about friendship, loyalty, decision making, and kindness. Are you looking for some material to get your little ones thinking about our big, complicated world we live in? Get your copy (print or ebook) of *Read-Aloud Stories with Fred, Vol 1*. today.

"Great stories! We very much enjoyed reading these short stories together. Each story gave way to reflection and interesting discussions with my 10- and 11-year-old boys."
~Lisa C., 5-stars on Amazon.com

The Dog and the Flea: A Tale of Two Opposites by Fred Olds (Coming in Fall 2020)

Flea moves about differently than any flea you've ever met before. But he still gives Doggy a huge, itchy issue. Now with both Doggy and Flea dealing with their own problems, what happens when the sun beats down on Doggy, and Flea gets too hot? Doggy's quick reaction just might save him some scratching in this fun, silly picture book by master storyteller Fred Olds. This book comes complete with illustrations by Robert T. Tong, Jr., and facts about dogs and fleas, plus a little activity on opposites.

Made in the USA
Monee, IL
08 July 2021